KU-753-117

Bing's Sticky Plaster

HarperCollins Children's Books

Round the corner, not far away,
Bing and Coco are **playing** today.

This Bing book belongs to:

...........01-2228411.....

ainse Mheal Ráth Luirc
harleville Mall Branch
01-2228411

ainse Mheal Ráth Luirc
Charleville Mall Branch
01-2228411

Copyright © 2023 Acamar Films Ltd

The *Bing* television series is created by Acamar Films and Brown Bag Films
and adapted from the original books by Ted Dewan.

Bing's Sticky Plaster is based on the original story 'Plasters' written by Gerard Foster, Lucy Murphy, Mikael Shields,
Ted Dewan and An Vrombaut. It was adapted from the original story by Rebecca Gerlings for HarperCollins *Children's Books*.

HarperCollins *Children's Books* is a division of HarperCollins*Publishers* Ltd
1 London Bridge Street, London SE1 9GF

www.harpercollins.co.uk

HarperCollins*Publishers*
Macken House, 39/40 Mayor Street Upper, Dublin 1, D01 C9W8, Ireland

1 3 5 7 9 10 8 6 4 2

ISBN: 978-0-00-855699-0

Conditions of Sale
This book is sold subject to the condition that it shall not, by way of trade or otherwise, be lent, re-sold, hired
out or otherwise circulated without the publisher's prior consent in any form, binding or cover other than that in which
it is published and without a similar condition including this condition being imposed on the subsequent purchaser.
No part of this publication may be reproduced, stored in a retrieval system or transmitted
in any form or by any means, electronic, mechanical, photocopying, recording
or otherwise, without the prior permission of HarperCollins*Publishers* Ltd.

All rights reserved

Printed in the UK

This book is produced from independently certified FSC™ paper
to ensure responsible forest management.

For more information visit: www.harpercollins.co.uk/green

Bing and Coco are at the coffee table, doing collage.

"**More sticky**, please, Flop!" says Bing.

"Here you are," replies Flop, passing him
another piece of tape.

It sticks to Bing's fingers, making him giggle. "Sticky wicky!"

Coco picks up a piece of paper that has fallen on the floor.

"OW-OW-OW-OW!"

she cries, snatching her hand away.
"I cut my finger! Oh . . . blood! It hurts!"

"Oh dear, Coco. It's a paper cut," says Flop.
"They can be painful, but we can sort it out."

"I need a plaster," says Coco.

"Which plaster would you like?" Flop asks.

"Erm . . . purple, please," replies Coco.

"Ooh!" says Bing excitedly. "Can I have the orange one?"

"No, Bing. You can only have a plaster if you're *really* hurt like me!" says Coco.

"Coco's right. Plasters are for when we really need them, Bing," explains Flop, wrapping a purple one around Coco's finger. "There, how's that?"

"Well, it still hurts," says Coco. "But it feels a *bit* better. Thank you, Flop."

"Oh, I can't do any more making now," sighs Coco as she sits on the sofa. "I need to rest my finger."

That gives Bing an idea. "Ooh!" he says. "I can be **Nurse Bing!**"

"Good idea," says Flop.

Bing puts on his stethoscope. "Now, tell me where it hurts," he says.

Coco sticks out her finger. "Here," she sighs.

"You're being *really* brave," says Bing.

"I know," replies Coco.

Bing is having trouble hearing through his stethoscope because Charlie is giggling so loudly.

"Charlie, shhh!" he says. "I need to listen . . ."

"Now I need to do the thermometer," explains Bing.
But . . . he accidentally knocks Coco's sore finger.

"Ow, Bing!" she cries.

"Sorry," says Bing.

"Careful of Coco's finger," adds Flop.

Bing takes the thermometer
from under Coco's arm
and checks it.

"Ooh . . . it's four o'clock!"
he says.

"That's the *time*, Bing!"
says Coco, laughing.

Next, Bing takes his hammer and boings Coco on each knee.

"Boing!" says Coco. "BOING!"

They both start to giggle.

"Good!" he says. "Now you're all better!"

It's time for Coco to be the nurse now.

"You lie on the sofa because you're *very* sick," she tells Bing.

"Ooh! Okay," says Bing.
"Can I have **a plaster?**"

"No, Bing," replies Coco.
"You can only have one if you *really* need one."

First, Coco listens to Bing through the stethoscope. Then she takes his temperature with the thermometer.

"Oh no! Four hundred million degrees!" she shouts.

"Oh, now I really, *really* need a plaster," replies Bing. **"Please?"**

"Oh, okay," Coco finally agrees.

She hunts through the nurse's case. "Nope, sorry," she says.
"There aren't any plasters in here."

Bing is disappointed. Then he remembers the
sticky tape on the coffee table. He has an idea . . .

"We could **make** one!" he suggests.
"We could use **the sticky tape!**"

Bing holds out his arm, ready for his plaster.

Coco carefully places a piece of
sticky tape on it and smooths it down flat.

"I've got
a plaster!"
Bing shouts,
running to
the kitchen
to show Flop.

"Bing!" Coco calls
after him. "I haven't
said you're better yet!"

"Look, Flop," says Bing.
"I've got a plaster too!
It's a bit tickly . . ."

"That's because it's
not a *real* plaster –
like mine," adds Coco.

"Oh, I see," replies Flop,
inspecting Bing's plaster.

"Is it okay, Bing?" Flop asks.

"Er, I don't like it, Flop,"
answers Bing. "It's all
itchy. Can you take it off?"

"I can try," replies Flop.

"OW!" shouts Bing
as Flop tries to peel it off.

"Oh, sorry, Bing . . . sticky things can hurt when you take them off," explains Flop.

Coco offers to help, but Bing wants to do it himself.

Bing tries to pull the sticky tape off.

"OWWWWWWWWWWWWW!

I can't get it off my arm!" he cries.

"Hmm, well, maybe you could take your arm off the plaster?" suggests Flop.

"Erm . . . how?" asks Bing.

Flop explains that they need to practise first.

"Put your arms up like a bird," he says, showing them.

Bing and Coco follow.

"Then flap them down."

Up! Down! Up! Down!

They all flap their arms together.

"Now," says Flop. "This time I'll hold on to the plaster. Uppp . . ."

Bing lifts his arms high in the air.

". . . and quickly – DOWN!" says Flop.

And . . .

off comes the sticky-tape plaster!

"**Oh! I did it!**" gasps Bing. "It is a *bit sore*, Flop!"

"Oh, let's see. I know what to do for that," says Coco.

Coco tears off a paper towel and wets it in the sink.

"I learned how to do this at big school," she says. "This will make it feel better."

Bing wraps the wet towel around his sore arm.

"Better?" asks Flop.

"Thank you, Coco!" says Bing.

"Good for you, Bing Bunny. You were really brave," says Flop. "And good for you too, Nurse Coco."

"Thank you, Flop," she replies.

Plasters . . . they're a Bing thing!
(But only if you really need one.)